ANNA RUSSELL

An imprint of Enslow Publishing
WEST 44 BOOKS™

Please visit our website, www.west44books.com. For a free color catalog of all our high-quality books, call toll free 1-800-542-2595 or fax 1-877-542-2596.

Cataloging-in-Publication Data

Names: Russell, Anna.
Title: What if / Anna Russell.
Description: New York : West 44, 2019. | Series: West 44 YA verse
Identifiers: ISBN 9781538382578 (pbk.) | ISBN 9781538382585 (library bound) | ISBN 9781538383292 (ebook)
Subjects: LCSH: Children's poetry, American. | Children's poetry, English. | English poetry.
Classification: LCC PS586.3 W446 2019 | DDC 811'.60809282--dc23

First Edition
Published in 2019 by
Enslow Publishing LLC
101 West 23rd Street, Suite #240
New York, NY 10011

Editor: Caitie McAneney
Designer: Sam DeMartin

Photo Credits: cover Michael Hall/Taxi/Getty Images; back cover (drumset) Ksanawo/Shutterstock.com.

Printed in the United States of America

CPSIA compliance information: Batch #CS18W44: For further information contact Enslow Publishing LLC, New York, New York at 1-800-542-2595.

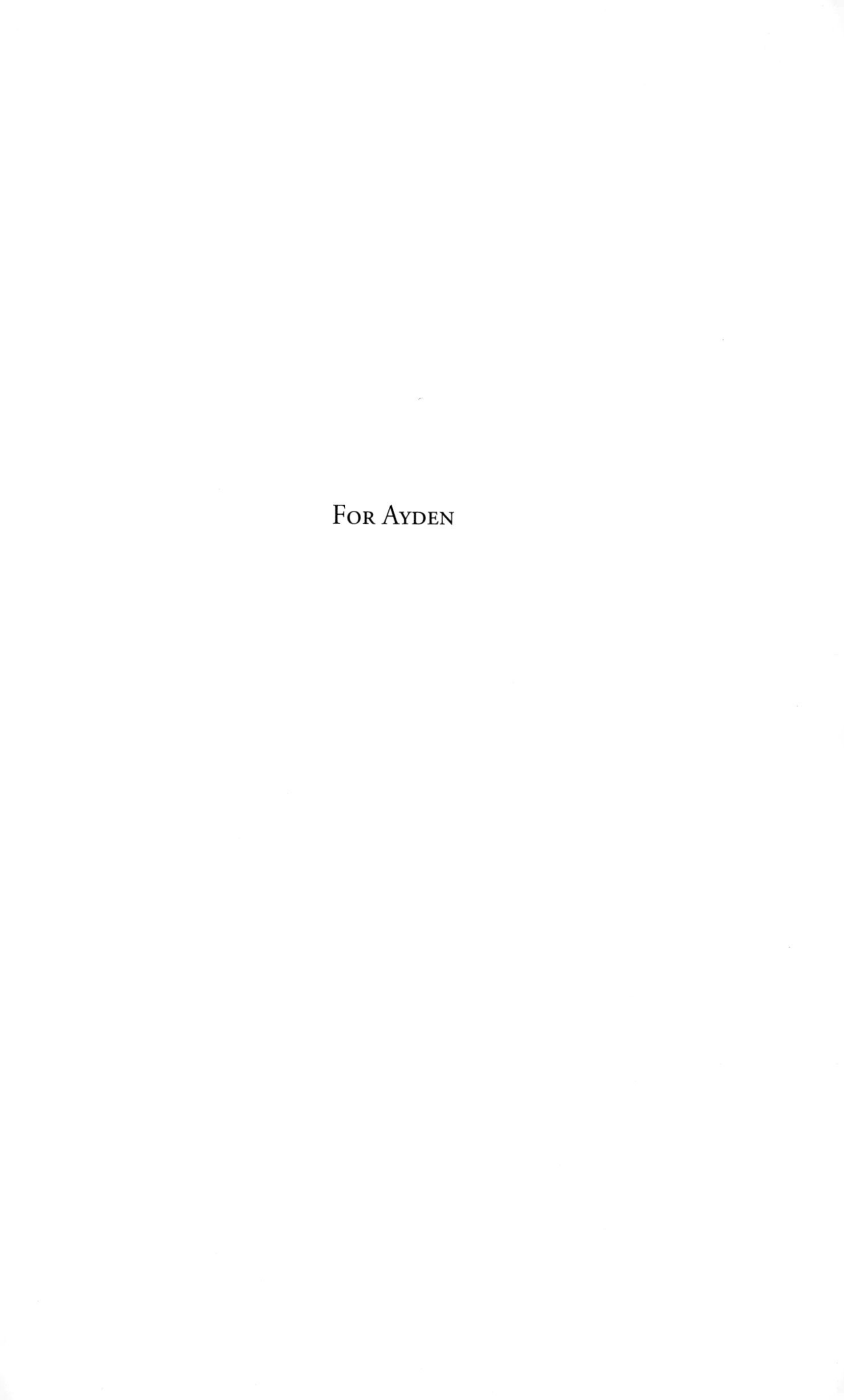

For Ayden

OFFBEAT: PART ONE

My thoughts don't bother me

here.

Drumsticks resting
between middle-finger
knuckle and my thumb.
Pointer finger

r e l a x e d

against the wood. I hit
the snare.

tap
taptaptap
tap
taptap

Marching band beats.

When I'm drumming, things feel

right.

Like finally fitting a puzzle piece
into its spot.

I AM

Joshua Baker.

Sixteen years old.

Future rock star.

The biggest

rock and roll fan

ever to live.

Training

for

perfection.

OFFBEAT: PART TWO

I feel the
rhythm
in my palm.

I close my eyes,
the song
building to the

best part:

the solo—

but I hear

a knock

at my bedroom door.

I feel sweat
between my eyebrows.

I can't:

speak,

lift my hands,

press pause.

If I don't finish,

The perfect puzzle will

fall

apart.

THE MANAGER

Dad walks in,
waving his hands at me.

He's like a manager.
Tells me which shows
I'm allowed to play.

I'm only the star.

Doesn't he get it?

I have to finish
this song.

"Joshua!" he screams.
I shake my head. My body

m

o

v

e

s

even though I don't tell it to.

Almost done, I try to say.
It has to be perfect, I think.

But Dad snatches a stick.

The

music

stops.

(My thoughts spiral.
Have to finish or Dad will hate me forever.
Must be perfect or Dad will make us move again.)

"You're gonna be late for school," Dad says.
Tucks the drumstick into his back pocket.

My lips when he leaves:
closed.

My mind:
You have to finish the song—or else.

Something *bad, bad, bad*

is going to happen.

I guess sometimes my thoughts bother me

here.

MY FIRST MEMORY

I'm three. Mom's
cleaning, as always.

Dad plays a Beatles album,
which means it's Sunday.

The song is "Blackbird."

I count to 10,
over and over.
Can't stop
until the song ends.

I don't know why.

My sister,
Julia,
scoops me in her arms.

Same blond hair as mine,
clear brown eyes like marbles.

She makes it better.

Now, I'm much taller
and we don't really hug.

But Julia might understand
the bad thoughts.

Maybe Julia will help.

(I need

to talk

to Julia.)

CAN YOU HEAR ME?

Julia sits at the kitchen table.
I can see her from the stairs.

Her headphones poof her hair
into a crown of pink curls.

Her piano fingers
mirror whatever she listens to.

I watch her pretend-play piano,
and imagine

what it would be like
to form a band.

No sound from her fingers.
My song, unfinished.

From up high,
I whisper, "Julia,"
as quiet as the music
she sends into the air.

But somehow,

she turns around,
smiles.

And for a second,

I forget I'm 16,
that it's not,

you know,
cool

to be friends
with your older sister.

But in this second,
I want to be.

A LIST OF NEW/OLD THINGS

New:

School.

House.

Drumsticks.

(My lucky ones were lost
in the move.)

Julia's pink hair.

(Mom promised she could—
a reward for moving.)

Dad's new advertising job.

(The way he's stopped
talking to me like we're buds.)

We moved closer to the city,
and it feels like
everything has changed.

Except:

Mom's dishrags.

Her triple chocolate cake.

Daily drum practice.

Two hours
of lessons.
One hour
for fun.

And the tugging
inside my stomach,

like being stuck
in the heavy
mud of a swamp
when I can't

control

(understand)

my thoughts

(my worries).

WORRY WARTS

At night, Mom used to say,

"If you worry so much,
you'll get worry warts."

But I couldn't

stop thinking.

Until:

1. I knew how many cracks
   were in the ceiling,
   counted them five times.

2. I checked my bedroom window.

   Unlock, open, close, lock.

   Check.

   Unlock, open, close, lock.

   Check.

   Repeat.

3. I mumbled all the words
to *Abbey Road*
without

messing

up.

After my shower each morning,
I check everywhere

for warts.

MY MOM

can dance tip-toed,
scrubbing away invisible
dust, dirt, and mold.

Spinning on knees,
or pushing the vacuum
over rugs.

As kids, when Julia and I couldn't
find her, we looked in the basement.

Saw her thumbing
through pages of past
birthday cards
and
artwork from
kindergarten.

"Why do you think she saves it?" I asked Julia,
during our move.
Boxes of our old papers
stuffed in the trunk.

The two of us waiting
in the car for Dad to fill
the gas tank
and Mom
to buy us burgers.

Julia thought for a moment.
Then said, softly,

"I think
she wants all
the pieces
of us—
who we used to be."

I looked out the car window,
saw Mom walking toward us,

sunshine-grin
lighting up her face.

"Julia?" I asked.

"Do you think that means
she's afraid
of who we're
going to
b e c o m e?"

Then, our parents came back in the car

and drove us

toward change.

I'M TOO OLD

to wave goodbye to Mom,
even though it's the

first day

at the new school

and

I

am

scared.

I get on the bus. And quickly,

so none of the other kids
can see,

I lift my hand,
give an awkward twitch.

Bye.

I can (maybe) stand it if Dad
doesn't like me.

(*Your fault, your fault,*
my brain says.)

But with Mom,

it would be much worse.

I look away like the cool, new kid
I'm trying to be,

but I hope she understands.

BEFORE WE START

"Why'd Dad have your drumstick
this morning?"

Julia asks,

her voice bouncing
as the bus hits
a pothole.

Before I can answer, she says,

"You know he just wants you
to focus on other
things."

But what else matters more

than the beat I create?

Her question

makes my swamp-stomach

come back.

I swallow a lump
down into my core
as my brain starts to say,

What if something happens?

It doesn't make sense,
but my thoughts say,

What if Dad gets hurt
because he has my drumstick?

Like some bad luck charm?

What if Julia starts to hate me
because I won't—I can't—
stop playing?

I breathe past the nausea
and start to hum
the end of "Hey Jude"
(na, na, na, nananana)

under my breath

making almost no noise,

until the bus pulls

into the loop.

Then, I fix my hair.
Smooth my clothes.

Maryville High School.

A
new
start.

HEAD DOWN

It's not the first day

for the other kids.

They know

where to go,
who's who.

Julia shrugs, says,
"What's the worst
that can happen?"

She skips to the 11th grade hall.

Gone.

And here I am:

head down,

trying my locker

over and over and over again.

Three to the left,
eleven to the right,
all the way around again.

I can't stop.

Even when the bell rings.

Even when I hear,
"That's the new kid, right?"
somewhere behind me.

Even when the English teacher
calls my name.

I run to the bathroom,

count to 20, 100 times,
and then 300 times.

When the door opens,
I panic.

But a man spots me,

says, "Are you Joshua?"

I nod, *Yes*, eyes down, can't
remember
how to speak.

"Do you like math?" the man asks.

And I look up.

GUITAR MAN

The man has funny glasses,

like little horns

tilting up from each eye.

I find out

that he is the 10th grade math teacher.

He keeps his hands

in his pockets as we walk

down the hall.

I think

if he were in a band,

he'd play guitar—

but not lead.

Not electric, either.

No, he'd keep it quiet, soft,

plucking notes just to himself.

He wouldn't force people to listen

to his songs,

but they'd want to.

FORMULA

My new teacher's name

is Mr. Maxwell—

like

the Beatles song

about the silver hammer.

He says, "Joshua, tell us about yourself."

I don't know what to say.

My lips, glued shut.

But then,

my fingers tap on my new desk

and I say the truest thing I know:

"I'm a drummer."

I even smile,
    just a little.

Mr. Maxwell nods and smiles back,

    and when he writes a formula
    on the chalkboard

        (numbers, x's, equal sign)

he calls on me,
    and I know the answer.

AT HOME

Julia talks
and talks

about her day:
books,

friends,

classes.

Dad says,

"Josh, what about you?"

I wonder

if he knows

that I didn't make it

to any classes but math.

I wonder

if he knows

what goes on

in my mind.

I wonder

if

we'd have to move again

if

he ever found out.

MAKING FRIENDS

Ringo,

from
the Beatles,

was my imaginary friend

in grade school.

Dad would tell me he was
nobody's favorite:

Beatle,
songwriter,
drummer.

But I thought he was a good listener.

Together,

Ringo and I

learned
beats,
songs,
uneven
rhythms
of
jazz.

I think, if he wasn't imaginary,
Ringo would help me find peace
at Maryville High.

Maybe he'd help
me to like it
a little
bit
better.

NOT EVERYTHING CAN BE SOLVED LIKE A MATH PROBLEM

Every day that week,

Julia and I

take the bus,

then go separate ways.

I think I hear some of the kids

whispering about me.

But they can't know

that I'm different.

That I worry if I don't do

what my thoughts

tell me, the people I love

might get hurt.

They can't tell. Right?

I look at my feet,

don't say a word

to anybody.

Who would like

a freak like me

anyway?

I feel better during math,

that *just right* feeling.

But after, I have English,
then social studies,
gym,
science.

And I don't

think

I can do this.

SHEET MUSIC

On Thursdays,
        I go to music class.

At this school, there's no
        marching band.

No music room full
        of drums to play on.

        Just:
                cymbals,
                metal triangles,
                one snare drum.

We all take turns playing.

        The instructor, Ms. Lions,

        sends me home with sheet music

for the winter concert.

"What about a full drum set?" I ask.

She puts both hands on her hips.

Her gray bangs cover her eyes.

She tells me that only seniors,

the oldest students,

can play the full set.

She packs a mini-xylophone into its case,

tells me to try that first.

Here's the thing, though:
I'm going to go crazy
if I can't play.

MORE THAN NERVOUS

The guidance counselor,
Miss Jones,

sends a note
to my homeroom,
asking to see me in
her office.

"Joshua," she says when I sit.
"Everybody gets nervous
about going to a new school."

I'm more than nervous, I want to say.
"'Kay," I actually say.

"You have to try
to get to all of your classes
on time, yes?" she says.

I want to tell her
that I can only

leave my locker
after opening
and closing
the lock
10 times.

I want to tell her
that I can only

talk in Mr. Maxwell's class.

I want to tell her
that I can only

do what my thoughts tell me.

But I look at her,
and I say,
"Okay."

NO NOISE FRIDAYS

At the end of the second week

at Maryville High School,

Julia finds me on the bus and pulls me to sit with her.

"They're going to call Mom and Dad,"
she says.

My palms start to sweat.

"Miss Jones told me to check on you.

Josh, do you understand?

You have to go to all of your classes.

Or else."

I don't want to think about

before.

But Julia looks angry, like

she still blames me

for having to move.

She's right.

But I know she won't tell
Mom and Dad.

Instead of fighting, I ask her
to practice with me—

something we haven't done
since we were kids.

It's the only way I can talk to her:

our silent band,

her invisible piano,

my no-sound drums.

She sighs, but we play through the entire quiet

of *The White Album*, part one.

We don't say much,

but after part one's over,

I hope Julia knows
I'm sorry.

IT'S MAGIC

I'm 362 seconds

late.

It keeps happening:

I have to, have to, have to—

turn my lock and
count to 100
at the same time.

My thoughts don't make sense.

When I open the door for English class,

everybody has a partner.

I sit,

I hide my head

in my arms.

I don't want to,

but I start to count.

(My heart slows.)

But then.

But then.

"Joshua?" a voice says, right by my elbow.

I lift my head.

"Need a partner?"

The voice belongs to a girl,

hair tight in braids,

deep brown skin,

sparkles on her lips.

"I'm Mage," she says. "I'm new, too."

When I open my mouth,
I realize I'm smiling
around my words:

"Um, yeah," I say.

She has a dimple on each cheek and blue braces.

I feel something change when she
sits by my desk

and says,

"Magical."

TODAY'S GOOD THING

In English,
we're the
perfect pair.

We finish our questions.

Mage knows all the answers
because she read *Hamlet*
at her last school

(and
she
is
the
smartest
person
I've
ever
met).

She shows me her drawings.

Cartoons, anime, portraits
of her dad and old friends
from Florida.

"We had to move," she says.
"After Mom. Cancer."

I keep my eyes down,
mumble, "Sorry."

"Yeah," Mage says.

"Are you okay?" I ask.

"Are you?" she asks.

And we both sort of sit there,

staying in that moment,

where we know the truth.

How

not

okay

things can be.

VISIBLE

After English,
Mage and I

walk to our lockers.

Her homeroom is just
down
the
hall

from mine.

(Was she one of the kids
who whispered about me?)

She has science next
and I have social studies.

But we still
walk together,

us,
new friends.

At least, that's what I think we
could be.

We stop at her locker first.

Mage unlocks her lock
with three quick moves.

She doesn't get stuck
the way I do.

I don't want her to see me
at my locker,

in case my need
to spin my lock
and count
makes me look

crazy.

My chest feels itchy.

The way she looks at me
is like I've just taken off
an invisibility cloak
and she can see through

every

part

of

me.

"Josh?" Mage asks,
touches my shoulder.

"I gotta go," I tell her.

She looks hurt,
eyebrows pinched tight.

I'm not who she thought I was.

"Where?" she asks. "You can't just leave."

Her science teacher hears
her loud voice.

He starts
to walk
toward us.

Toward me.

The other kids look at me,
laughing into their hands.

I think about what
they would say

if they knew who I was—

if they knew exactly
how different I am.

My body tenses
until there's only one thing
          I can do:

I run.

AWAY, AWAY

When I lived in the country,
every corner was a
hiding place.

Our neighbor had
cows, horses, and a sheepdog.
Trees lined the space

between our backyards
like a toothy smile.

Space was unlimited,

i n f i n i t e.

When the swamp-stomach,
and the thoughts,
and the worry warts
were just too much,

I'd sneak past the
wood's grin
to a special tree
with a knot tucked
in its bark.

Time stopped.

It was away from everything.
Like I was away
from myself.

NOW, IN THE CITY

all the trees are bare.

I don't know where to go

when everything is too much.

So I walk

and walk

and walk.

THE MOVE

Last school year,

I messed up.

My grades dove
into the ground
and didn't come back.

To be fair,

Dad warned me,

said,

"Joshua, there will be
consequences
if you don't improve
your schoolwork."

I didn't think it'd go this far.

Dad was offered a fancy
marketing job in the city,
but he couldn't decide:

should we leave everything
just for his career?

What about us, his kids?

Then, he got a call
from the school.

Josh is failing
his freshman year,
the principal explained
to my parents.
He'll have to repeat a grade
if he's going to stay at
this school.

And my father—
who was the first
in his family
to graduate from college,
the first to manage a company,
the first to be able to teach
his children what success
meant to him,
what

he

expected

from

us—

packed us away.

I helped make his decision
all too easy.

Because of me, our family will never be the same.

JULIA, THE TELLER

I knew I'd be in trouble.

I mean,

I sprinted
from school.

Left

through
the front door.

I was ready

to be grounded,

I was ready

to hear Dad yell.

But I wasn't ready

to see Julia standing there,
pointing right at my chest,

saying,

“There he is. There he is.”

FOUND

I didn't get too far this time,
just looped around our
neighborhood
a few times—

702 steps.

When my parents find me,
they take me home
in our white sedan.

I'm in the backseat with Julia,
but I sit as far away
as possible.

She's on their side now?

She called them.
She told my secrets.
She told them
        everything.

BEHIND GLASS

You know how

when you go to a museum,

they have animals,

polar bears and mountain lions
and the smallest of birds

stuffed and propped?

You'll stare at them,

maybe just a little afraid
that if you blink, they'll
come to life again.

That's sort of what it's like
at school the next day.

I'm the animal, frozen.

Everybody—
even the teachers—

watches me,
unblinking,
to see if I'll thaw,

come

undone

and start to move.

They know they can't

stop me

if I do.

TO BE SEEN

Before English class,

(before I have to see Mage again)

I have a meeting with

Mom, Dad, and Miss Jones.

We sit at Miss Jones's table
and she asks me what happened.

I look at Dad

and I don't want to say
anything about my thoughts.

But when I look at Mom,

I think that maybe
she'll get it. Maybe?

"Sometimes," I say.
"I can't control my thoughts."

The adults look at each other.

I swallow past a lump
in my throat,

and then I confess everything:

the counting,
the songs,
the worrying.

Nobody speaks for a

long

time.

Not until Miss Jones asks me
if I would step out into
the hallway.

When I slink
out the door,
press my back to the wall,

I can just hear them talking
to one another.

Dad asks, "What does this mean?"
Mom asks, "Is he okay?"

I imagine Miss Jones takes a breath,

before she says,

"I think Joshua

needs

to be seen

by a specialist."

ODDBALL

When Mom and Dad leave,

Miss Jones walks me
to English.

(If she didn't,

maybe I'd disappear again.)

Mage is already there,

sitting
at
my
desk.

She stands when she sees me.

My face is flaming.

"Welcome back," she says.

I rub the back of my neck.

"Still partners?" she asks.

"You want…?" I start to say.

She shrugs.

"Maybe you're a big oddball,
but normal people
bore me," she says.

"Thanks," I say.
"I guess."

"It's okay," she says, laughing.
"I'm weird, too."

With Mage, things feel…

not perfect—

but like

they don't
need to be.

OUR LANGUAGE

There's only one

thing left

that hasn't

been fixed.

Julia.

We've barely spoken since yesterday,

since the car,

since I knew that my secrets

weren't mine anymore.

I was upset,
at first.

But what's done is done.

Julia and I sit together
on the bus ride home.

We're quiet,

until I tap two beats on her knee:

It's okay.

She looks at me,

and she understands.

A NEW TRUTH

Mom wakes me up the next
day with a pen and papers
in her hands.

"We set up an appointment
with a psychiatrist," she says.

Miss Jones's words
come back to me:

I need
to be
seen.

"They want you to
fill out this form
so they can learn
a little about what's going on.
Answer the questions
truthfully," Mom says.

My mouth feels dry.

It's time for truth.

A KIND OF PERFECT

As I'm falling asleep that night,

I remember

when I was really young.

The memory is fuzzy
like I can only see it
through half-closed eyes.

But I make out the shape
of Mom. We're in the kitchen,
and it smells like winter:

gingerbread and chocolate
on the stove.

Then, there's a

crash.

Mom drops the whole tray
of cookies onto the floor.

Dad runs in, saying,
"What happened?"

Mom,

crying into Dad's chest,
screams,

"It has to be perfect."

She redoes the cookies
over and over and over.

I don't think she could ever
make them the kind of perfect
that's in her head.

Why'd we never talk
about this moment?

Because *that's* how I feel.

THE BIG DAY

I sit in the waiting room with Mom.

The walls look like peppermint candy.
She reads a magazine. I count
the wallpaper's stripes.

A man comes out of a door
down the hall
and he shakes our hands.

He says his name's Dr. Sprout.

He has a salt-and-pepper beard
and talks like he's got
a laugh stuck in his cheeks.

He says, "Let me show you
my office."

But when Mom gets up with me,
Dr. Sprout says,
"Sorry, just Joshua today."

Then, we're alone.

His office is emerald green.
Smells like old tea bags.
But the air feels

        different

in there.

Like maybe

        it wouldn't be too hard

to tell the truth.

THE HONEST, WHOLE TRUTH

These thoughts have been here,

in my mind,

for as long as I know.

I tell Dr. Sprout

that I remember

always needing

that

just right

feeling,

ever since I could think.

Ever since

my thoughts

could control me.

It's like slowly

s i n k i n g

in quicksand,

staying just above the grains,

always a second away

from

drowning.

I tell Dr. Sprout that

1. I have to count
every crack in the ceiling

or else it'll fall
and kill everybody.

2. I have to check
my locker
again and again

or else somebody will take
my lunch money.

3. I have to sing
songs in order
on *Abbey Road*

or else Julia will get sick and die.

4. I have to finish
my drumming
exactly right

or else my swamp-stomach
will come back
and never go away.

He listens and doesn't
call me crazy.

He listens and he tells me
it's not my fault.

He listens and says,

"Joshua,

have you ever heard

of something called

obsessive-compulsive disorder?"

INTRUSION

When Mom comes in,
Dr. Sprout explains:

"Obsessive-compulsive disorder,

OCD for short,

makes people's brains, their thoughts,

get stuck

and worries

seem bigger.

OCD thoughts are

intrusive.

Like if you're

trying to tell a story

but in the middle of a sentence,

somebody keeps blowing

a loud horn.

All you can think about

is the horn.

Then, the only way

to make the sound vanish

is to do what it wants.

If that horn will only

s t o p

when Joshua counts,

again and again,

that's what he's going

to do.

This is called a compulsion.

It makes the bad feeling

better,

but only
for a little
while,

so you want to repeat what
you did to make it go away.

Those intrusive thoughts,

the loud noises,

won't ever

disappear.

But with time
and practice,

it'll be easier

to tune out the horn

without giving in
to what it wants."

My head feels filled
with fog.

Then, Dr. Sprout
makes out a prescription
for medicine.

SIDE EFFECTS

At home, Mom explains OCD
to Dad.

He rubs his hands
over his face.

Sighs like his lungs
are filled with bubbles.

Julia and I exchange looks.

Dad doesn't think
I need the medicine.

"Well, just stop yourself
from doing
the—what are they called?

The rituals. Yeah. Rituals.
Now that you know,
can't you just...stop?"
he asks.

I feel heavy, like I'm strapped down
by an anchor. I'm a ship,
motionless.

Mom isn't sure about the medicine,
and what it will do, either.

But that night,
she's the one who brings me a glass of water,

smooths my hair,

and hands me the pill.

STARTING OVER

At first,

I didn't think
I was any different.

I had this thing—

OCD.

I took this pill—

for anxiety.

The first few weeks,

I still checked,
and double-checked,
and triple-checked

my lock.

Still counted
and started over

and counted
and started over.

Then, six weeks later,
just as I'm about to give up,
something amazing
        happened.

Picture:

        Me, all swamp-stomached.

        Me, counting the syllables to
                "Here Comes the Sun."

        Me, about to miss English.

Then, I tried something different.

I took a deep breath.

Whispered, "They're just thoughts."

And

        my brain

                stopped

                        counting.

LOOKING UP

I've seen Dr. Sprout
a few times now

and I feel almost kind of

normal.

The thoughts
haven't

d i s a p p e a r e d,

not completely.

But

it's getting easier

to shut them out.

In English, Mage says,

"You seem different."

We have our books

fanned open
in our hands.

Picking quotes to use
for our group project.

(Oh, yeah,

Mage

and me?

Partners for everything now.)

“Different?” I ask.

“Yeah,” she says.

I feel my face
get warm.

“Different how?”

Mage looks at me for a
long
time.

I wonder what she sees:

my too-long bangs,
my holey Pink Floyd shirt,
callouses on my fingers
from gripping drumsticks.

Then, Mage smiles her big, all-teeth grin.

"You look

happy,

Josh Baker."

And I do.

I am.

ROCK OUT

As I am stepping
out of the door in math,

Mr. Maxwell says,
"Josh? Can I speak with you,
just for a moment?"

Uh-oh, I think.

We took a test
earlier in the week.

Maybe he's going
to tell me that

I failed,

or that

he's disappointed.

In moments like these,

the swamp-stomach
comes back.

Mr. Maxwell hands me
a green sheet of paper.

It's folded in half,
and when I unfold
it, the title reads,

in big, block letters:

TALENT SHOW

"You should think
about performing," he says.

"I hear you drumming
on the underside
of your desk.

It's time to let the rest
of the school
hear you rock out."

I don't know
what to say or think, but I tuck
the flyer into my pocket.

ERASED

I let my body

become the rhythm.

tap taptap tapraptap rap
thud thud crash

My limbs are now
base and cymbal and snare.

The drumsticks

know where to move.

I'm not playing
a particular song,

no sheet music.

It's just

every part of me,

of who I am,

in drumbeats.

I’m playing too loud,

and too fast,

but I am

just right

here.

As I play out the end,
adding fills, yelling

out all the bad thoughts,

I see somebody in my doorway.

Jaw dropped,

eyes wide.

I fumble,

my drumstick soaring

across the room.

There,

like she appeared by magic,

in my house,

listening to me play
my
heart
out

is Mage.

AN AUDIENCE OF ONE

"Dude," Mage says.

She keeps saying it.

Her mouth won't close.

I'm all red:

tomato-head,
rose-cheeks,
fire-hot.

Because

besides Mom, Dad, and Julia,

and people in band class,

nobody has ever

heard me play.

Especially not like that.

"Dude," Mage says again.

“I…” is all I can say.

“That was magic!” she says.

“How are you here?” I ask.

(But I’m happy she’s impressed.)

“We had plans,” she says.
“For our Shakespeare
project, remember?”

“Oh,” I say.

“Forget about the project!”

Then her face
glows, like she
is a whole,
beautiful moon.

She says,

“I have the best idea.
A wonderful,
magical, best idea.”

OUR PACT

There, in my room,

(once I'm more relaxed)

we make a pact.

The two of us

are going to

start

a band.

I'll be drums. She'll be guitar.

"I didn't know you played," I say.

"All jazz, baby,"
she says.

"You want to play
in front of people?"

She nods,

only frowning when

she realizes

we don't have a gig.

Then, it's my turn
for a suggestion.

I think about the talent show
flyer, still pocket-crumpled.

"Well," I say,
suddenly finding
the courage to tell her.

"I might have an idea."

Those words are like locking pinkies—
a promise.

LISTEN

Mage stays
for dinner,

　　and everyone
　　seems to like her.

I learn new things
about Mage.

　　Like how she's
　　a vegetarian.

(She eats her spaghetti
without meatballs.)

And how she's never
seen snow.

After we clear

　　our plates,
　　Dad brings out

his acoustic guitar,
which he hasn't

　　played since the move.

When Mage
takes the guitar
in her arms,

she looks
complete.

Like it's a part
of her:

mind, body,
and soul.

WILL IT WORK?

The next day,

I tell Dr. Sprout
about Mage—

how she plays
like she's made
of music.

He grins,
and we talk a lot
about my thoughts.

He says,

"I see,"

whenever I say that I
think the medicine fixed me.

At the end,
I mention the talent show.

"Please," I say.
"Please make sure
the medicine works
when I do this."

Dr. Sprout presses his lips
into a tight line.

Our time is up for today,
but he tells me to practice
breathing exercises.

And, as I'm leaving,
he says,

"Remember, Joshua, you don't
need to be fixed—
just helped."

OPPOSITE FORCES

When I come out of Dr. Sprout's office,

Mom is in the waiting room.
Twisting the hem
of her sweater

like
a
pretzel

between her fingers.

She's been extra quiet

today.

It's the kind of silence

she gets when she meets
somebody new.

(But she knows me,
right?)

We walk out the door together,

climb in the car.

One of us should speak.

She goes first:

"Josh?"

"Yeah?"

Here it is, I think.
Here's the moment
where she'll say
she doesn't know
who I am
anymore.

Then,

"Can you describe it?" she asks.

"What?"

"The thoughts," she says.

"Uh."

How can I do this?

How can I show how
my thoughts,

all those

what-ifs

take over?

I repeat what Dr. Sprout said:

the loud noise,

how it won't stop

unless you do what it wants.

Mom isn't driving.

We sit, motor running,

in the parking lot,

and she

listens.

I see her swallow.
I see her bite the inside
    of her cheek.
I see sweat gather
    where her bangs
    are parted.

"All you want," she says,
"is for it to feel right."

"Yeah," I say.

"And when it doesn't,
you feel like two magnets,
opposite forces,
pushing everything inside
of you

a p a r t."

My mouth opens.

In the corner of my vision,
    I see Dr. Sprout's
holiday lights blinking

red, blue, green.

I look at Mom.

"How did you know?" I ask.

She closes her eyes for a moment.

(Julia and I look like
Dad, except
our brown eyes,
and the dimple
above our top lips.
We're like Mom
in those parts.)

"Just a guess," she says suddenly.

Then she starts the car and
turns a Rolling Stones song up
all the way
until I can't hear my
own thoughts.

TWO PATHS

The next week,

the day before winter break,

none of us can sit still.

We're all jitters,
all ants-in-pants,
the if-I-don't-get-
out-of-here-now-
I-might-explode
kind.

In English,

Mage rests her cheek on her palm,
dozing.

("I call it meditating.
I'm Zenned out," she says.)

She watches the frost gather
on the window.

Then, suddenly,

Mage gasps. "Look!"

And there it is: the first snowfall.

After that,

nobody can talk about
Shakespeare.

When the bell rings,

we're all out of there.

It's sort of the same
as when I ran out of school.
But the pings in my belly
bounce around happily.

And I'm not the only one
who runs this time.

The entire 10th grade
is outside,

tongues out
to catch flakes
of ice, chins
tilted toward
the sky.

Eventually,
we go back.

Mage waves goodbye to the snow,

eyes bright,
smile wide,
crystals still caught
in her braids.

This is
happiness:

a light, airy feeling.

Worries: an almost-silent hum.

A feeling like I'm going the right way.

I find my desk in social studies,
plop down.

Bliss.

Then, Mr. Wright
hands me my
graded paper
and another path
opens in front
of my eyes.

THE WRONG PATH

I feel heavy, dark,
like I've swallowed
a starless night sky.

I got a C-

on the essay.

Not good enough for Dad.
Not a grade Julia would have gotten.

I think back to writing it:

how I had to start over
to get it to feel right,

how I had to make it perfect
but how I knew it never would be.

My thoughts play on repeat:

Any grade lower than a C

has to have a parent signature.

This is not good.

My stomach bubbles. My head aches.

Quickly, under my desk,

I sign Mom's name in cursive
on the top of the essay,

and tuck it away where nobody can see my secret.

HARMONY

The first day of winter break,

Mage comes over again,
this time with her own guitar.

Together, we decide we'll need

Julia's help,
her keys,
her voice,

to really pull this off.

(I'm still not sure
if I can play
in front of people.)

Julia agrees right away,

says, "Let's show them what we've got."

She floats in and out
of different songs
while we try to choose

what to perform.

"A Beatles song, right?" Julia asks.

Mage wrinkles her nose.

"You don't like the Beatles?" Julia says.

(To her, this is betrayal.)

"Well," Mage says, her face
scrunched up.

"I grew up with more jazz
and soul.

Otis Redding, Aretha
Franklin..."
she says,

her gaze going slightly
out of focus,

like she's somewhere
else. Not cross-legged

on my bedroom floor.

"They're fuller," she says.
"Have more heart."

We start simple:

a few chords,
notes held out,
a simple pattern
on my drum.

At one point,
Julia and Mage sing
in perfect harmony.

"Whoa," I say.

The girls look at each other, smiles growing.

I know what Mage will say
before she opens
her mouth:

This is magic.
We are magic.

BAKER DAY

My family doesn't do normal holidays.

We have our own:

Baker Day,

even though it's really
a three-day celebration.

This year, Dad takes off of work,
and Mom makes the schedule.

Day one: We make cookies and
take them down to
the homeless shelter.

We bring a pot
of apple cider,

with cinnamon
and cloves

mixed in.

Our warmth,

for others
who need it.

Day two: We go to a local farm,
just to look at the trees.

We don't chop one down,
but Julia and I cut a branch

from a spruce,
brush the pine needles

away, tuck
the fresh smell of winter
into our coat pockets.

After, we just
drive,
through the countryside,

down by the creek.
We take a picture

here. The water
is frozen, so we stand

on the ice, laughing,
breathless, because

it could break
beneath our feet

at any point.

At the end of the third day,
we sit with our new presents,
lazy, bellies full

of turkey and green beans,
and
Mom's triple chocolate cake.

Then we bring out our instruments.

Day three is my favorite day:

playing, without worry,
as loud as we can.

We're a family
of musicians:

Mom's singing,
Julia's piano,
Dad's guitar,
my beats.

I hadn't realized
before, but

I get it now:
my family,

they were my
very first

band.

CATCHING RHYTHMS

The day before school starts again,

Mage comes over,

brings her composition notebook,
black-and-white squiggles

filling the cover.

"My music book,"
she says.

She opens it

and I see hand-drawn
sheets,

lines straight,

and notes
e v e r y w h e r e.

They are pencil markings on paper,
but I can hear them.

"So here's what
I'm thinking," Mage
says.

She sits in her usual spot

on my bedroom floor.

Right below the place
on my ceiling where
there's a cluster of
glow-in-the-dark stars.

A reminder of my old home.

"What if we did
a medley of
our favorites?"

"That might work,"
Julia says, closing her eyes,
already thinking.

"Josh," Mage says,
turning her head
to look right at me.

"You've been quiet."

It's only been a little while,
but it seems as though

Mage knows

how to read

me.

"Sorry," I say to Mage.
"Just..."

"Lost in thought?"
she says.

"Something like that," I say.

A worry comes

into my head,
and I don't like it.

It says,

If you tell her
the truth,

if she knows
about the thoughts

and the counting
and the worrying,

Mage will never
want to be your

friend or
be in your band.

I zip my lips,
tight.
I don't tell anyone,

not Mage, not Julia,

even though Dr. Sprout

told me to share
my thoughts.

Instead,

I sit,
I play,
and I pretend

that I'm a normal

drummer,

only worried

about catching
each rhythm,

and getting it right.

SET LIST

We practice until
we can hear
each note

without touching
our instruments.

We'll play a combo of:

1. "Superstitious" by Stevie Wonder
   (For Mage, who joked,
   "Josh, you're sort
   of superstitious, right?"
   If only she knew.)

2. "Only the Good Die Young" by Billy Joel
   (For Julia, her favorite
   song on piano.)

3. "The End" by the Beatles
   (which has a drum solo)
   (which I have to play)
   (by myself)

A mishmash, sort of like us.
The perfect, imperfect band.

PRIORITIES

We rest our hands.

Stretch our fingers.

Pause practice for the day.

Mom orders pizza,

half pepperoni, half mushroom.

When Dad comes home,

his footsteps are heavy,

like he could fall

through the floor

and wouldn't care.

Sometimes, he has days like this

when he doesn't make

his marketing goals.

Tonight,

he says,

"Welcome, Mage.
You and Josh
finish that Shakespeare project?"

She swallows, tells him,

"We're getting close."
Even though we haven't
started yet.

He nods, brushes his hands

together.

"Remember, school
comes first,"
he says.

Then, he looks at me,

"Got it?"

I think about the C-,
my face starting to turn red.

He doesn't know,
I tell myself.

Julia,

as though she's picked up

on my thoughts,

looks my way

and sends a secret message:

Don't mess this up again, Josh.

CRAZY

We go back to school
the next day.

(Great.)

It's not so bad:

Mr. Maxwell brings us
sour gummies.

The insides of my cheeks
feel like they're pinched
together for the rest
of the period.

But he tells me after class
that I'm falling behind.

I haven't told anybody

that when I do homework,

my thoughts tell me to:

1. rip up the page
(because it won't ever
be good enough);
2. erase and rewrite
over and over again

(because what if
my teacher
can't read my
answers,
and I get
an F?); and

3. don't turn in anything
(because I'm not
smart enough
to get a good grade,
anyway).

The quarter
will be ending

in two days,

and it's too late
for me to fix

these problems.

LOSING MY COOL

In English,

Mage and I use free time
to gather quotes
for our project.

We're writing about Hamlet
and Romeo,

comparing the ways

they lost their

cool—

lost their

minds.

"Did Hamlet really see ghosts?"
our teacher asks.

"Was he hallucinating?

Was this

mental illness?"

Mage thinks the topic
is fascinating.

But I feel jittery inside,

maybe from the candy,

but something else, too.

"So what do you
think?" Mage asks.

"About what?" I ask.

"Do you think
Hamlet went insane?"

"I don't know," I say.

"C'mon, Josh,"
she says.
"Was he crazy?"

I remember,

back in Dr. Sprout's office,

confessing
that, sometimes,
I felt

crazy.
Out of control.
Irrational.

I don't see ghosts,

but I use rituals to make
worries go away.

Am I as bad as Hamlet?

Am I as bad as Romeo,
who let love,
his worries,
drive him mad?

I feel a sort of
pang,

like lightning,

go through my spine.

I slam my book shut.

“Does it matter?” I snap.

“Uh,” Mage says.

I wish I could take it back.
I wish I could hit rewind.

I wish, I wish—

but it’s over.

I yelled at Mage.

That urge to *r u n*
becomes so strong,

I don’t think I can fight it.

But then,

Mage places her hand
on my shoulder.

“Tell me,”
she says.

She knows
something
is wrong with me.

UNDONE

Mage's house is
cozy,

which is the word Mom tells me to say
because it sounds better than small.

But it's just the two of them:

Mage and her dad.

She starts to lead me
upstairs.

"Uh," I say.
"Does your dad let…
boys
in your room?"

She laughs.
"Pop trusts me,
and respects
my space."

I rub my hand on the back
of my neck.

"He'll be home soon,"
she says.

Until then,

it's just us,

and, even though
I am fully clothed,

I feel exposed,
like I'm out naked
in a snowstorm.

"So, uh," I say.

Mage motions with her hand
for me to continue.

She sits cross-legged
on the floor,

like she does in my room.

"It's okay," she says.

"I have this thing," I blurt out.

It's all coming out:
obsessive-compulsive disorder,
the thoughts,
all the *what-ifs*.

As I'm telling her about it,
it happens
right on cue.

What if Mage won't understand?

What if she won't want
to be friends,
partners,

anymore?

What if I sound crazy,
like the characters
in Shakespeare?

What if
I *am*
crazy?

These worries

make my brain
think it needs
to count

to 100,
backwards,

at least 3 times.

If I do that,

maybe everything
will turn out
okay.

I close my eyes,

my secrets
hanging
in the air

between us.

Here,

in Mage's bedroom,

her purple walls,
polka-dot comforter,
drawings everywhere,

I come undone.

All of me
for her to see.

After a moment,

I open my eyes again.

(I only counted backwards
from 100 once.)

She looks at me,

her head tilted to the right
just slightly,

her lips pressed
together,

eyebrows pinched
toward one another.

Say something, I think.

"Wow," she says.

"Yeah," I say.

"You have those
thoughts all the
time?" she asks.

I shrug.
"Not always,
but, like,
a lot at school,

and when I do
something new,

and…" I hesitate.

"The first time
we met," she says.

It's not a question.

I can tell

she's remembering
me by her locker.

Me, sprinting away.

"Sometimes," I say,
"the thoughts
are all I can hear."

"What do they sound
like?" she asks.

I think for a second.

"Like a million
chords in minor
are being played
all at once," I say.

"And they only go
away—"

"If I do what they want."

We sit quietly for a long time.

Suddenly, I need
to tell her one more thing:

"I'm the same
person you
first met," I say.

"I'm even better
about the thoughts
now.

But I get it
if you don't want
to be my partner
anymore."

She blinks at me,
and then

her mouth
tilts up.

Smiling, as bright as the sun.

"Dude," she says.
"I'm your partner
no matter what."

SIDE A

Only minutes later, Mage's dad
comes through the front door.

"Up here, Pop!"
Mage calls.

I stand up, brush
my hands down
my jeans, smoothing
invisible wrinkles.

It's not that I
like Mage
like *that*.
(I think.)

But I think
she might
be my
best friend,

and I want Mr. Robinson
to approve of me.

Once he enters the room,
I stick my hand out.

"It's nice to finally meet you,"
he says.

Finally—like Mage
has been talking
to him about me.

I learn that Mr. Robinson
doesn't play any
instruments.

Mage got her interest
and talent

from her mom.

Mr. Robinson puts on a record
(real vinyl, an old
record player)

and we listen while we eat
French toast and pancakes.

Mage is just like him:

always smiling,
laughs at anything,
pure joy.

Maybe I expected
lines around his eyes,
or his face to be stuck
in a frown,
still mourning
Mage's mom.

Instead,

he replays
side A
of the record.

He leaves it on,
playing to
an empty room

when he drives me home.

It makes me imagine
that this was Mage's mom's
favorite.

That even when bad things happen,

even when the room is empty,

there can be happiness
left over
in the grooves

of music.

INTERMISSION

In the car with them,

I get a good feeling,
comfortable. Warm.

And I wonder

if this is what some people

feel like

all the time.

Here, I am in a snow globe.

Everything drifting softly, slowly.

I hug Mage goodbye.
I shake Mr. Robinson's hand.

Then, when I step inside my home,

I see my father standing,
back to the living room window,

a paper clutched in his fist,

and my world shatters.

ONCE BEFORE

When I was eight and Julia was eleven,

she had her first big piano recital.

She was jumping with excitement

for weeks, had a sparkly dress picked

out and everything.

She was so focused

on practicing

that she forgot to finish

a book report.

Dad found out,

and Julia wasn't allowed

to play for a whole month.

EAR WORM

It's not a bug—

it's when a song,
or a phrase,

just gets stuck

in between the folds

of your brain

and you can't shake it out.

In my head,

on repeat,

is:

It's over.
It's over.
It's over.

SIDE B

"Can you explain this?"
my father asks,

turning to face me.

I've never seen him
this red.

Scrunched-up nose,

A big, blue vein
pressing against

the skin of his forehead.

I can't speak.
All I've done is stare

at that paper,

wondering what it could
possibly say.

"This, Joshua,"
Dad says.

"Your progress report."

Oh, I think.

My dad is sort of like

Mr. Robinson's records:

    there's two sides to him.

The first:
    kind, goofy,
    Beatles-loving,
    musician
        (the kind
        who understands
        the need to play).

The second:
    this version,
    wanting us
    to always
    be better.

"This is unacceptable,"
he says to me.

He shows me the sheet.

Math: C
Science: D
Social Studies: F
English: D

I think about the nights

I don't talk about,

sitting awake,

head pounding,

because I

c a n ' t

be perfect,

and that makes everything harder.

"Dad," I say, not sure
what else I can do.

"You put all your energy
into those drums,

and now into
the band

and that girl,"

he says.

"What did I tell you
about school?

It needs to be your
priority, Joshua."

"It is,"
I squeak out.

"This doesn't show that,"
Dad says.

"Dad, it—it's OCD."

He scoffs, a harsh
sound in the back
of his throat.

"Not an excuse."

I feel as though

I've swallowed
a handful

of heavy stones.

He folds the paper
back into a square,
and puts it in his shirt pocket.

"You're grounded,"
he says. "Until
these grades

all say A or B."

"Grounded?" I say.

"No drums," he says.
"Except for school."

"The band—" I start to say.

He shakes his head.

"No band. No talent show.
No Mage. Got it?" he says.

I think about having to move
again, or worse—

some sort of boarding school
for troubled kids.

I think he'd do it.

He is ready to take away

everything.

For once,

the worries were completely right:

it’s all over now.

AWAKE

I don't sleep that night.

I count. I hum. I repeat Beatles albums

over and
over again

in my mind.

What am I going
to tell Julia?

What am I going
to tell Mage?

HOW TO LIE

I almost don't show up
to English.

It would be

so much easier

to give up,

to run away.

But if I ever

want to be friends

with Mage,

and have a band,

I have to get

an A.

"Josh?"
Mage says.

It's just my name,

but I feel like
I could turn
into nothing but tears.

"You asked to have
a different partner?"
she asks.

I think I'm drowning,
or sinking, or
being sucked up
into a hole.

"Yeah," I say.
I can't look at her.

"Why?"

For a moment,
I think about what it would
feel like

if I told her the truth.

But I'd have to admit
to the grades

and being yelled
at by my dad.

I don't want her to look at me

like
I'm
crazy
and
stupid.

So, I make up a story.

"I decided it's better
if I work by myself," I say.

"We're too different,"
I say.

"We can't help
each other," I say.

They're all lies,

and she believes
each one of them.

"What about
the band?" she asks.

I take a deep breath,
hold it in my lungs,

and tell the biggest
lie yet:

"There's no point.
We're not good enough."

Mage stays quiet.
She turns her head
away from me.

"You're a very
different person
than I thought."

I watch as Mage walks
to the other end of the classroom.

All I can do is stare

and wait for her

to hate me.

JULIA, THE SEER

I've been quiet,
no sound,
for two whole days.

On the bus going home
by the end of the week,

I rest my head
against the window.

Julia sits by me,
doesn't say much,
just leans back

and closes her eyes.

I do the same,
and eventually she opens
her lips:

"I saw Mage today."

I concentrate on my breath:

one to five, breathe in,
hold for seven seconds,
release for five seconds.

"Joshua," Julia says.

"I think you should talk

to Mom."

What good would that
do? I want to ask.

Instead, I just
b r e a t h e.

It's always been Julia and me,
like we were twins—
the same heart,
the same soul.

"Trust me," Julia says.

SUNDAY SECRETS

I don't sleep anymore.
    I read for school.
    I study.
    I write.
    I erase.
    I redo.
    I try—

but something else happens
in the hours when the sounds

of Julia's piano practice

grow quiet

and I stop tapping
drumbeats with

my pencil on paper.

In these moments,
I can hear my parents.

Sunday night,
they talk

    about me.

"I had to, Mary," Dad says.

From the other room,
their voices sound
as though they're
traveling

through a tunnel
made of copper.

"He's miserable," Mom says.
"How is that going to help?"

I hear a creaking noise
and I can picture

Dad pacing across the floor.

"He needs to try," he says.

There's a pause.

"I think that's where you're
wrong," Mom says.

"Josh is already trying."

TUNE-UP

Maybe I should be nervous
to tell Dr. Sprout that I'm
failing.

And that Dad grounded me
from doing
what I love
most.

But when I walk into his office
on Wednesday, I feel as though
my lips
have been
unlocked.

I tell Dr. Sprout about Dad
and Mage
and the band.

I tell him what it'll take to be able
to stay in this city.

I can't get shipped away.

At the end, I tell him what Julia
said about Mom.

He listens, posing
with hand under chin,
his “I see” look, full-force.

When I’m finished, he writes
something down on a notepad.

Rips off the sheet,
hands it to me.

“That is for an increase
in the medicine you take,”
he says.

“Sometimes it’s about
finding the right dose.”

Then, he sighs, squints his eyes
at me, and nods his head.

“There’s something else, Josh.

What you said last time,
that you thought you needed
to be fixed—

the medicine will help
you to manage
those worries, the thoughts.

But it won't make them go away
forever.

OCD is like a rusty, old car,

and the medicine is just
a routine tune-up.

But, Josh, you are in control

of the car.

Some days, it will sputter
and maybe
lose power.

But if you work at it, it'll get you

wherever you want to go.

With enough love, it could grow wings,

take you
beyond
the moon.

You have to be honest with the people

around you.

You have to tell them when you need a ride.
Because that rusty, old car is just too tired
to move on its own.

You have to tell them so they can help you
to push it uphill.

You don't

have to

do it

alone.

Do you understand what I'm saying?"

Dr. Sprout leans forward in his chair,

examining me so close,

I think he can hear my every thought.

I nod back to him,
stand,

let his words

sink
in.

"Talk to your father," Dr. Sprout tells me
before I leave.

"Let him see the work you've put in."

He's right:

I have to talk to Dad.

I have to make him

understand

the parts of my brain

that

get stuck.

No matter what he thinks.
No matter what he'll say.

COME CLEAN

Just like last time,

Mom lets the car run
in the parking lot.
And we sit

together.

She says, "I want to tell you something."

And when her lips part,

everything
changes.

MOM'S STORY

"I knew I was

different

when I was five," she says.

"We were making stained-glass
hearts as presents to give
for Mother's Day.

I *needed* it to be perfect.

You see,

my mother was pregnant
with your Uncle Jordan,

and on bed rest.

At night, I had to rub her feet
to help the swelling.

They would hurt her so bad

she couldn't walk.

After massaging them, I'd
wash my hands

until they were

raw.

Thinking that if I didn't,
my feet would swell up, too.

I wanted to do something nice for her.

I wanted to make her
feel better.

I remember

in class,

everybody else was laughing,
smiling,
swirling paint together.

But I didn't understand.

Because my whole body

was shaking

with effort to color in the lines.

To have it look
neat.

My heart felt as though
it was going to

burst

through my chest.

All I kept thinking was,
*If this isn't perfect, Mommy
won't feel better.*

That thought repeated

on a long loop
in my mind.

I took one look at the little glass figure.

To anybody else, it looked fine.

But to me,

it wasn't
good enough.

I picked it up.

It felt so fragile between my fingers.

I imagined my mother opening

this imperfect heart.

And I
couldn't
take it.

I lifted my arm

and threw it

on the ground.

It shattered into tiny, glittering pieces.

My heart, my worries,

turned to sharp glass at my feet…

what I'm trying to say, Joshua,

is this:

I think I understand."

IMPERFECT HEART

As soon as we pull into
our driveway,

I'm gone:

> into the house,
> up the stairs,
> to the music room.

I have the drumsticks
in my hands

> before I even know
> what I'm doing.

I think about Julia,

> always watching her grades
> so that she would never
> have to sacrifice music.

I think about Mage,

> and how the rough
> guitar strings
> beneath her fingers
> let her visit
> her mother's memory.
> With music,
> she can make it through.

I think about the band,

and how happy
I was. How everything
seemed to be falling
into place

and falling apart
all at once.

I think about Mom,

how her worry warts
are invisible,
and how she can't
be perfect,
even when she tries
her best to be.

I think about Dad,

and I know he'll understand,
eventually.

Then,

I play.

CRESCENDO

Everything builds:

the thoughts

(*taptap taptaptap taptap*)

the what-ifs

(*raptaprap boomtaptap*)

the rituals

(*one-y and a two-y and a one-y*)

the fear of failing

(*tssh tssh crash*).

Right here

tucked between drumbeats is me:

rule breaker, OCD mind, math whiz, band member.

I am...   just who I'm supposed to be.

HEAR ME

Dad calls my name,

loud,

from downstairs.

He heard the drums,

but can he hear

what I'm trying

to tell him?

"Before you say anything,"

I say to him once I walk

down the steps.

"I need you

to hear me."

It takes a long time,

minutes, or hours, or years,

to really explain it all.

To capture that

not right

feeling,

and get him

to understand.

I wonder

if Mom told him

her story

because he stays

quiet.

Doesn't interrupt.

Just

listens.

"I know that it doesn't

seem like I have

good grades,

or that I pay attention

and do my best,

but, Dad," I say,

closing my eyes,

squeezing them shut

like I'm making a wish.

"Please understand

that I'm trying

harder than I ever have.

I don't want my brain

to get stuck like this.

I don't want to

disappoint

you."

I wasn't sure

what to expect
after revealing
everything.

I thought my father

might send me off
to a different school

or

raise his voice,
louder than thunder,

or

(worse)

say that he would never
understand my OCD.

I never would've guessed
that Dad would sit down
and pat the seat
next to him.

That he'd exhale softly,

finally looking at me,
and whisper,
"I'm sorry."

DAD'S SONG

Once, when I was small,
five years old,

Dad took me
to a record shop

way out in Ohio,
where he grew up.

It took four hours
to get there,

and on the way,
we listened to

the pop-twang
of the Beatles.

A road trip
with just Dad—

to me,
it meant everything.

The faint sound of
drums and electric guitar

greeted us. The store smelled
old, like dust and wet books.

"My dad took me here
when I was your age,"

my father said,
kneeling to my height,

"and I picked out my very first
record," he said. "I want you

to get whatever you want."
He looked so proud,

stood there tall, shoulders back,
looking around at the old shop.

And I knew it was my job
to make this moment for him.

I didn't quite get why this moldy,
run-down shop made him so happy.

Or why we drove so long just for this.

But I did know that it was my turn
to listen to him.

He was telling me about himself
that day. He wanted me to understand him.

Now, almost 10 years later,

it's him that makes the choice
to understand, even if he doesn't

quite get it. He sits there,
and he hears my song.

NO LONGER A SOLO ACT

The four of us,

me, Mom, Dad, and Julia,

squish together on the couch,

forearms touching, no space to hide.

I tell them that Dr. Sprout

wants to talk

to my teachers to explain

why it's extra hard

for me to do the things

that my classmates can do.

Julia says she'll help me

with science homework,

and Mom says she'll check over

my essays.

Dad says,

"We'll make a schedule

for schoolwork."

Julia squeezes his arm.

"Band practice?" she asks.

He nods, then looks at us,

and a smile lifts his cheeks.

"I guess that makes me band manager," he says.

We groan, shove at his shoulders,

pretend we don't want him to get involved.

But deep down,

all I can think is,

At least I'm not alone.

MY PARTNER

That night, I think of Mage.

Her mouth turned down,
eyebrows pulled together.

And I hear her saying,

You are a very different
person than I thought.

I have to make it up to her.

I have to prove
that I'm not

the person I pretended
to be.

Even though it's late,

I step into Julia's room.
She has her headphones in,

plugged into her keyboard.

"I need your help," I say,

She smiles, and together, we create.

TRACK ONE

For once, I get to English
early.

I place the disc on Mage's desk.
It catches

the glint of the sun, creating a rainbow.
I rub my palms

together, wipe them off on my jeans.
But it's a good

kind of nervous—a dance in my stomach.

I move to the back.

I wait for Mage to see my apology:
a mix of some of her

favorite songs, covered by Julia and me.
Drumbeats created

on bongos and Julia's keyboard programmed
to sound like a guitar.

I sang for the first time. I don't sound like
Julia, or the singers Mage

enjoys, but I know that when Mage listens,
she'll hear me. The real me.

TRACK TWO

She finds me after class.

"Did you make this?"
Mage asks.

I nod, knowing she hasn't
listened to it yet.
Wondering, wondering,
what she thinks it is.

"Why?" she asks.

"I was wrong before,"
I say.

"You said—"

"I know," I say.

"I didn't want you to know
the truth. My truth."

"I thought you told
me everything,"
Mage says.

"Listen to it," I say. "Please."

TO BE FREE

Later, my parents and I have a meeting

with all of my teachers.

I smile when I see Dr. Sprout,

who winks and takes a seat

across the table from my father.

Miss Jones asks me to start.

Even though I've done it a lot by now,

I still get nervous to explain

all of my thoughts. Everybody listens, taking notes.

In the end,

we come to the conclusion that I

might get what's

called a 504 plan that will let me

have extra time on assignments

and tests.

For the times when my mind

becomes extra-stuck.

When we start to pack up

to leave, Mr. Maxwell comes to my side.

"I'm proud of you," he says.

I feel my face grow warm,

and I mumble, "Thank you."

"I hope I get to see you play," he says.

And for a moment, I'm confused,

until I remember that next Friday

is the talent show.

I take a deep breath and say,

"It'll rock."

FORGIVEN

At home,

I get a single text from Mage:

"This mix is magic."

I send her a message back,

"I'll explain anything
you want to know."

"When?" she writes.

"Band practice at six?" I say.

"I'll be there."

And, just like that,

without needing to count,
without needing an OCD ritual,

I become the luckiest 16-year-old

in the whole city—

maybe all of the world.

THE BAD, THE GOOD

We play
with everything we've got:

our broken hearts,
troubled minds,
shiny, new souls.

Here,
as a band again, we are
safe in the rhythms we've made.

I can't help
but think of the bad.

(What-ifs, broken-record
thoughts, worry warts
that I'll have for
the rest of my life.)

And the good.
(Perfect beats, Mage,
my family, held together
by beautiful notes.)

And the
balance
between it all.

LUCK

The night before
the talent show,

Mom brings me
cookies and milk.

Like I'm a kid again.

I think she's been
happier, too,

because they aren't
perfect circles.

She asks, "Nervous?"
and I can't lie.

She smooths down
my hair, and says,

"You don't need
to do anything for luck.

It's all in your heart."

And I think she's right:

all I need is trust in myself.

I WAS

Undone, taken apart, examined,

and reassembled.

Afraid, overcome by thoughts.

I believed I *was* my OCD.

Sometimes, it feels like I'm barely

stitched together.

But instead of hiding,

I

will

perform.

BODY AND MIND: IN SYNC

The day of the show, Mage looks at me,

gives a thumbs-up.

And Julia squeezes my hand.

We take our places

on stage.

There's this feeling—

a tugging

deep in my gut.

Like I'm attached

to a string.

Being pulled

somewhere.

I let my mouth

go dry.

Let my hands

grow damp.

Let my thoughts

scream,

"What if."

Before letting

it all

go.

Then,

the curtain

rises.

I clink my sticks

together

(*clack clack clack*)

and everything starts on my count:

one, two, three.

WANT TO KEEP READING?

If you liked this book, check out another book

from West 44 Books:

SOME GIRLS BIND BY RORY JAMES

ISBN: 9781538382530

EVERYONE HAS A SECRET IN HIGH SCHOOL

At least, that's what
my older brother, Steve, says.

Some girls date
"bad boys."
Sneak out their windows.
Run off on motorcycles
with dropouts.
("You know," he shrugs.
"Like in the movies.")

Some girls ask:
"Hey Mom, Dad,
can I have some friends
over to watch Disney movies?"
Mickey and Minnie are harmless.
But they always wear gloves.
Maybe it's so they don't
leave fingerprints on
their parents' wine bottles.

Some girls play
spin the bottle,
around and around it goes.
But I don't know.
I've never met anyone
who has actually played.

ONE
too many
LIES
L.A. BOWEN

SOME GIRLS
BIND
RORY JAMES

The
Same
Blood
M. AZMITIA

Dreams on
FIRE
Annette Daniels Taylor

ABOUT THE AUTHOR

Anna Russell is a writer from Buffalo, New York. She received a degree in English and creative writing, and it is her goal to create stories for readers of all backgrounds and abilities. She has experienced OCD within her personal life, and she hopes to bring awareness about mental health to literature.